10 Minutes to
SHOWTIME

10 Minutes to
SHOWTIME

By Tricia Goyer
Illustrations by Maryn Roos

Tommy
NELSON®
www.tommynelson.com
A Division of Thomas Nelson, Inc.
www.ThomasNelson.com

Published in Nashville, Tennessee, by Tommy Nelson®, a Division of Thomas Nelson, Inc.

Scripture taken from Luke 2:14 of the New King James Version. Copyright © 1979, 1980,
1982 by Thomas Nelson, Inc. Used by permission. All rights reserved.

Library of Congress Cataloging-in-Publication Data

Goyer, Tricia.
 10 minutes to showtime! / by Tricia Goyer ; illustrations by Maryn
Roos.
    p. cm.
  Summary: A group of angels behind a curtain in the sky prepares for a
big debut over the manger in Bethlehem.
  ISBN 1-4003-0470-9 (hardcover)
  1. Jesus Christ—Nativity—Juvenile fiction. [1. Jesus
Christ—Nativity—Fiction. 2. Angels—Fiction.] I. Title: Ten minutes
to showtime!. II. Roos, Maryn, ill. III. Title.
  PZ7.G7483Aae 2004
  [E]--dc22

                                    2004010964

Printed in the United States of America
04 05 06 07 LBM 5 4 3 2 1

To my children, Cory, Leslie, and Nathan,
who opened my eyes to the wonder of Christmas.

Mommy loves you.

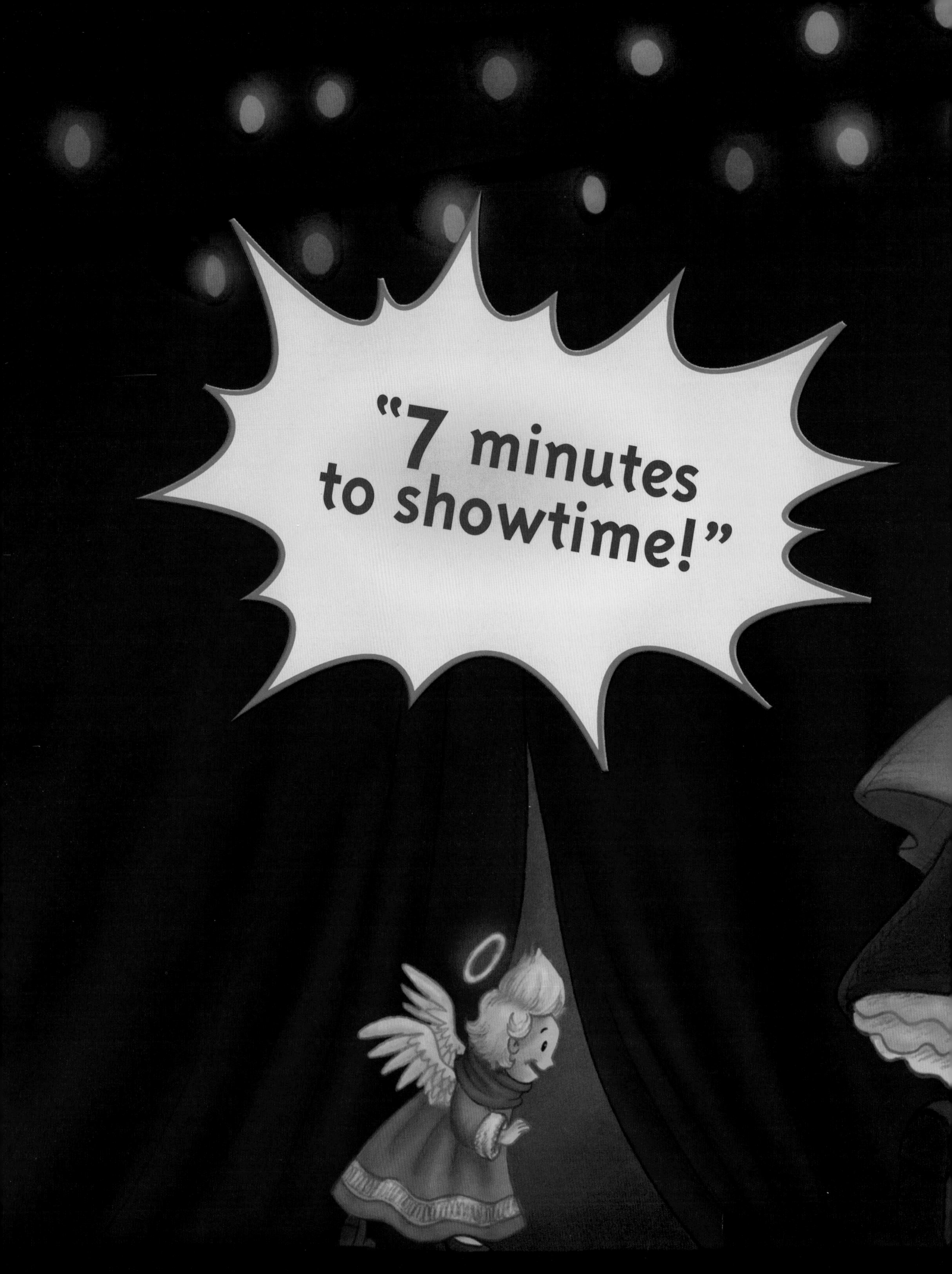
"7 minutes to showtime!"

"It's time. It's time!"

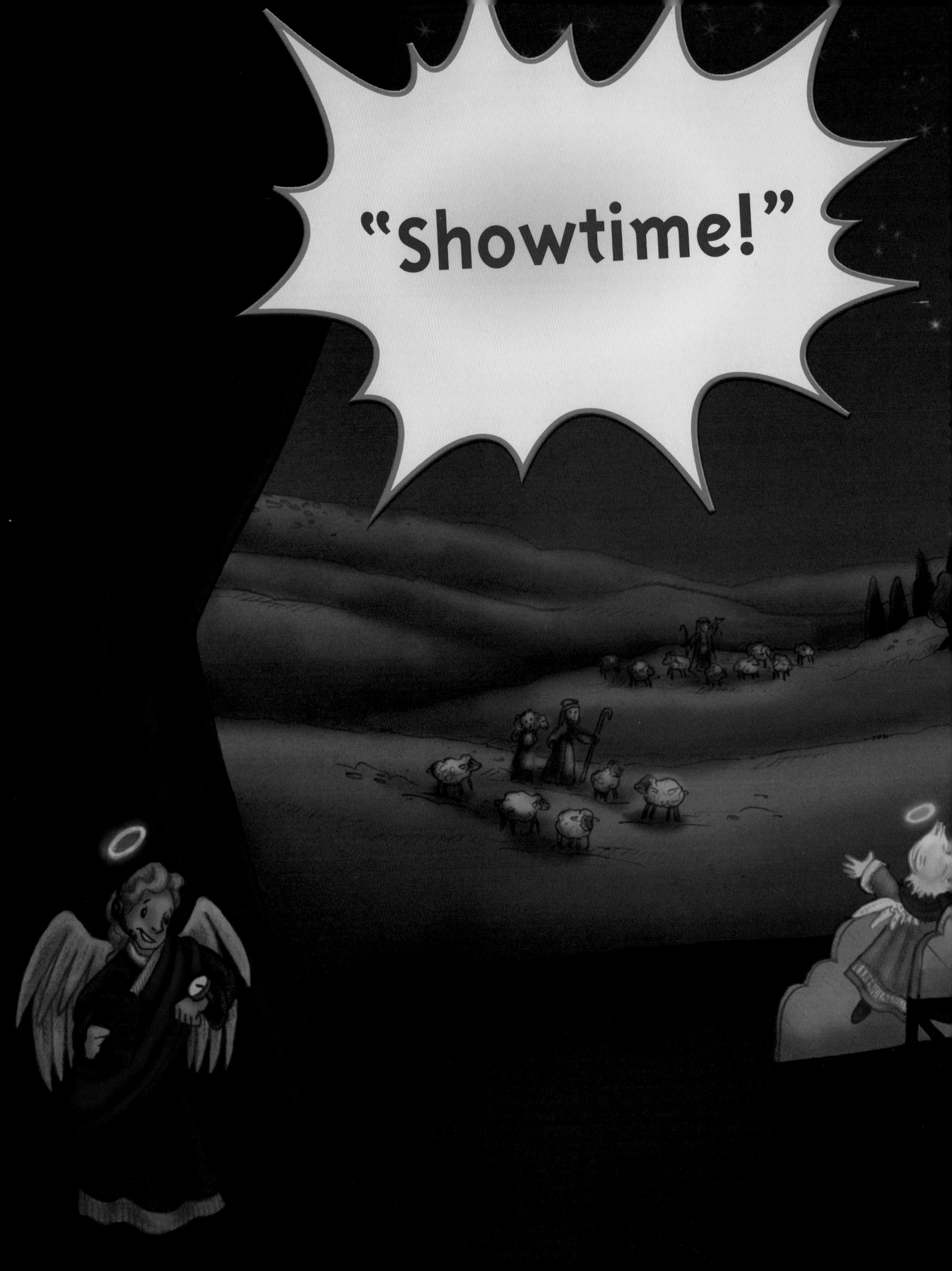
"Showtime!"

"He's such a miracle. I sense that all of heaven is rejoicing with us right now."

"I think you're right, my sweets."

Did you see those chubby cheeks?

"Did you see all that dark hair sticking out?"

"Wow, he has his father's eyes."